This is a work of fiction. Names, characters, places, and incidents either are the product of the author's imagination or are used fictitiously. Any resemblance to actual persons, events, or locales is entirely coincidental.

ISBN: 9798674188155

Copyright © 2020 by Eleni Charalambous
Illustration copyright © 2020 by Cynthia Bifani
First Edition September 2020

Cuddle in a Bubble

Cuddle in a bubble : Little girl on lockdown
Written by : Eleni Charalambous
Illustrated by: Cynthia Bifani

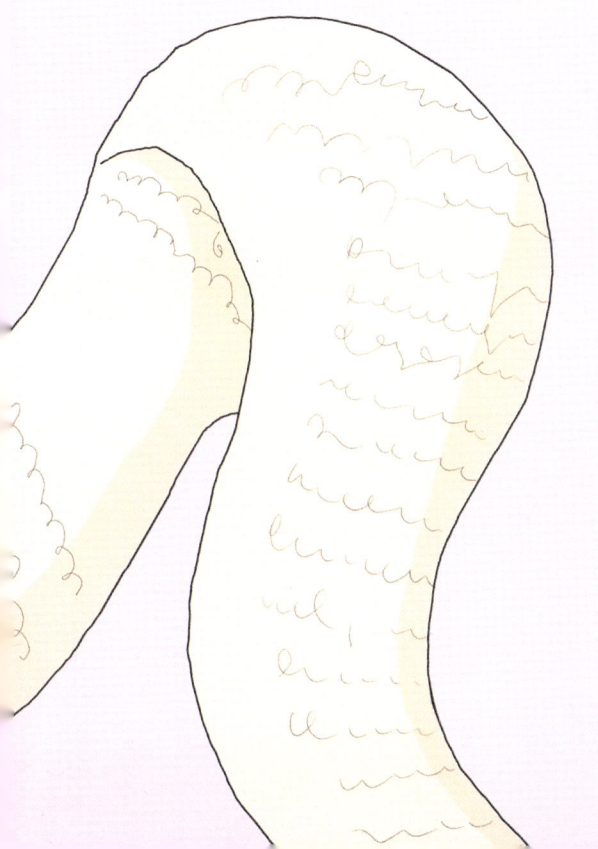

This book belongs to:

_____

_____

Who was ____ years old during lockdown.

I was quarantined with _____

To my Quaranteams who made lockdown a memorable one.

"Can I have a cuddle please?"
"Only if you can cuddle in a bubble."
A cuddle in a bubble?
Now, this just doesn't make sense.

So she thought and she thought,
but why can't I just have a cuddle?
"Haven't I been good to you?"

"It's not because you have been bad,
that is what makes this so sad,
but you need to be safe and sound,
so for now there will be no cuddles going around."

"If I can't have a cuddle, can I go and see Grandma?"
"Ok, but we can only see her through the window!"
"Why? Does Grandma not want to see me?"

"Definitely you she wants to see,
but the world has become a bit complicated for a while,
and you can't see the ones you love, even for a cup of tea."

"Mummy this makes no sense to me.
I feel that life has gone topsy-turvy.
When will we be back to normality?"

"We don't know yet my dear,
as there is something out there that's causing fear.
So, we need to stay home,
and not think too much about where we can't roam."

"Instead, we need to think about what we can do,
to make the ones we love feel that we still love them too.
Remember, near or far, short or tall,
we have so many ways to share love, maybe with a video call?"

"No matter what happens,
we should continue to think of ways to share our hearts.
Remember, it's always about kindness and love,
and that can be done in many ways, and not just with hugs."

"Maybe make a call?
Maybe send a letter?
Maybe think of all the ways that we can make this world better?"

"In time things will be better, but let's never forget the love that we can show."

So she thought and she thought,
and started writing lists of things she had been taught.
Let's start with BE KIND,
and let's never forget the pieces of love we can find.

Thank you to my First Quaranteam: Mum,
Dad and Yiayia who made the lockdown an experience I won't forget.

Demi, thank you for waving to me via the window when
days seemed too long.
Sophia for your long FaceTime chats.

Cynthia for having the talent to bring my character to life.

Niels, who continued to keep my spirits high during this time.

The Bonne-Hillewaere family for treating me like part of the family and
accommodating me during the second part of the lockdown.

Tanja for all of your expertise to finalise this project.

To all of my online students who helped me through
the days of lockdown.

I am forever indebted to all of my students who constantly continue
to inspire me and give me character building ideas.

Lockdown would have been impossible without all of
my wonderful family and friends in London and Cyprus who
entertained me endlessly with animated voice and video calls.

Eleni, British born with love for all things rhyming,
written and pun-related.

She gained a BA in Fashion Journalism in 2010 in London where her
love for writing continued to blossom.

She continued her Education by travelling to Greece in 2016
where she became TEFL certified.
She has since travelled to multiple countries volunteering and teaching
English to children around the world, which has
consequently led to her inspiration for writing poems for children.

Always looks for the good in everyone and always
believes tomorrow will be better.

Author's previous work:

Available on Amazon!

My Quarantine Diary.

_____
_____
_____
_____
_____
_____
_____
_____
_____
_____
_____
_____

Printed in Great Britain
by Amazon